MW00964249

Lilly's Special Gift

Lilly's Special Gift

Brenda Bellingham

Illustrated by Clarke MacDonald

First Novels

The New Series

Formac Publishing Company Limited
Halifax

The development and pre-publication work on this project was funded in part by the Canada/Nova Scotia Cooperation Agreement on Cultural Development.

Formac Publishing Company Limited acknowledges the support of the Cultural Affairs Section, Nova Scotia Department of Tourism, Culture and Heritage. We acknowledge the financial support of the Government of Canada through the Book Publishing Industry Development Program (BPIDP) for our publishing activities.

We acknowledge the support of the Canada Council for the Arts for our publishing program.

Library and Archives Canada Cataloguing in Publication

Bellingham, Brenda, 1931-
      Lilly's special gift / Brenda Bellingham ; illustrated by Clarke MacDonald.

(First novels ; 32)
ISBN 0-88780-665-1 (bound).—ISBN 0-88780-664-3 (pbk.)

      I. MacDonald, Clarke (Clarke Robert) II. Title.
III. Series.

PS8553.E468L553 2005   jC813'.54   C2005-902334-1

Formac Publishing Company Limited   Distributed in the US by:
5502 Atlantic Street   Orca Book Publishers
Halifax, Nova Scotia, B3H 1G4   P.O. Box 468 Custer, WA
www.formac.ca   USA 98240-0468

Printed and bound in Canada

Table of Contents

1
The Bracelet

I'm invited to Minna's birthday party.
So is Theresa. Minna is my very best
friend in the whole world, and I want
to give her a truly awesome present. So
does Theresa. Theresa is my second
best friend. She has the same problem
as I do — what to give Minna.

My mom says she'll take us to the
shopping mall. She has to go to the
supermarket there. Theresa and I can
window shop while Mom buys
groceries. We arrange a place to meet
after she finishes. My little brother,
Macdonald, wants to come with

Theresa and me.

"No. You come with me, Mac," Mom says. "I need a man to help me decide what to buy for supper. Pop's working late, so you're my man."

Mac looks as if he won't buy this story. Finally he does. Phew!

Most of the stores at the mall sell clothes. We don't want to give Minna clothes. There's a store that sells crafts and other neat things, like Beanie Babies.

"Minna's got too many Beanie Babies already," Theresa says.

"But I know she really likes them," I say. "Let's go see if they have any new ones."

On the way, we pass a jewellery store. It's on a corner and open to the mall. There is only one window. In the window I see a gold and silver bracelet. It looks like braided chains with diamonds sprinkled along it.

"Wait," I call to Theresa. "That bracelet would be perfect for Minna. She could wear it when she plays the piano."

Minna is going to be a concert pianist. Her teacher makes her give lots of concerts. I would die. Minna is very shy, except when she plays the piano.

For concerts, Minna has to wear a pretty dress — no jeans allowed. Usually the dress is long with short sleeves.

"That bracelet would look perfect on her bare arm," I say. "I wonder how much it costs."

"If you have to ask, you can't afford it," Theresa says. "That's what my mom always says."

2
Math Lesson

"I'm going to ask anyway," I say, going into the jewellery store. "That bracelet is awesome. Minna would love it."

Theresa follows me in. The clerk behind the counter is not a clerk. His name tag says he's the manager.

"May I help you?" he asks. He sounds polite, but frosty.

"I'd like to see that bracelet, please." I point to it. "I can't see the price."

"No." He looks down his nose. "We don't put tags on high-quality pieces."

"Why not?" I ask.

"Anyone could walk by and see the price. Usually someone buys a bracelet like that to give as a gift. You don't want someone to know how much you paid for a gift. It's not good manners. It's ... well ... tacky. It's the thought that counts, not how much you paid."

"I won't tell Minna the price," I say. "She plays the piano at concerts. The bracelet would sparkle when the lights shine on it."

"Did you say 'Minna'?" the manager asks.

I nod.

Now he looks more friendly. "I've heard her play at music festivals where my son has played the clarinet. Minna's very talented." He smiles at me. "The bracelet would make a lovely gift. But it's one thousand dollars, plus tax. I hope your piggy bank is full."

When an adult says something like that to a kid, it's called teasing. If a kid says it to an adult, it's called being sassy.

"Lilly doesn't have much in her piggy bank," Theresa says. "Her parents aren't rich. They drive an old Chevy."

It's true, but she didn't have to tell him. "How much is the tax?" I ask.

The manager explains. "It's seven cents for every dollar the item costs. So multiply one thousand times seven. That makes seven thousand cents, right?"

I nod. He should know. He manages the store.

"How many cents in a dollar?" he asks.

"One hundred," Theresa answers. She's good at math.

"So to find out how many dollars in seven thousand cents, we divide by one hundred. I'll tell you an easy way to do that."

I can see he likes math. I'm glad I'm not his son.

"I know how," Theresa says. "You cross off the last two zeros in 7000. That makes 70. So the tax is seventy dollars."

"Very good," the manager says. "Add seventy to one thousand dollars and you get one thousand and seventy. That's the total cost."

"Thanks," I say. "I'll think about it."

After we leave the store, I grumble to Theresa. "He made me mad. I wanted the bracelet, not a math lesson."

3
Minna's Worth It

It's Saturday and I have to find Minna a birthday present. Her party is this afternoon.

"I need a box of peaches for canning," Mom says. "We'll go to the Farmers' Market. We can look for Minna's gift, too."

"The Farmers' Market? You want me to give Minna a turnip or a cabbage? She doesn't even like vegetables — except Chinese, the kind her grandma makes."

"Calm down, Lilly," Mom says.

"They sell other things, including jewellery. Maybe we'll find a bracelet."

"Can't we go to the jewellery store in the mall?" I ask.

"No," Mom says. "Theresa's right. We're not made of money." I already told her what Theresa said about our old Chevy.

We go to the Farmers' Market. First we get the peaches, then we look at the jewellery stalls.

There are bracelets made of tiny beads. Bracelets made of big, glass beads. Bracelets made of coloured wire. I don't like any of them.

"Look at these," Mom says. She stops at a stall that has cubes with a letter on each one. "We can buy the

cubes and make Minna a name bracelet. She'll like a gift you make for her yourself."

"The cubes don't sparkle," I say. "They aren't made of gold and silver, and they don't have diamonds."

Mom sighs. "Lilly, you're being difficult. We can't afford gold or diamonds. Find something else."

"There!" I squeal. "That's the one I want. It's just like the one in the jewellery store."

A young woman wearing glasses sits in the stall. She smiles. "This one? It's my newest design."

It has a price tag, but it's too small to read. "How much is it?" I hold my breath.

"Twenty dollars," the woman says. "Would you like to try it on?"

"It's not for me," I say. "It's for my friend. She plays the piano. I want her to wear it when she gives a concert. It'll sparkle in the lights."

"I'm afraid it's a little more than I want to pay," Mom says.

"My husband's a pianist," the woman says. "Tell you what. For your friend I'll reduce the price to fifteen dollars."

"Please, Mom," I beg. "I'll give you five dollars from my piggy bank."

Mom hesitates.

"Minna's worth fifteen dollars," I say.

Mom smiles. "Every penny," she agrees.

We buy the bracelet.

4
The Birthday Party

I can hardly wait to give Minna my gift. Mom finds a little jewellery box she doesn't need anymore. It makes Minna's bracelet look even more beautiful.

Besides Theresa and me, two other girls come to the party. Sara is from Minna's church choir. Dana is from her Saturday morning Chinese school. First we go to a movie. We come back to Minna's house for munchies and birthday cake. Before we eat, we give Minna our presents. She spins a bottle to decide whose to open first.

Theresa is first. She gives Minna a towel that turns into a bag for your swim things. Neat. Sara's next. She gives Minna a nifty shorts-and-top set in really bright colours. Dana gives her a cool CD. Minna likes all her presents.

I'm last. Minna opens my gift and gasps.

"It's awesome," she says. "It's the most beautiful bracelet I've ever seen. Thank you, Lilly." She gives me a big hug. "I'm going to wear my bracelet for the rest of the party."

Theresa frowns. When it's time to eat, she doesn't sit beside me. "I'll sit over here by Sara," she says. She scowls at me across the table.

What's wrong with Theresa? Maybe

she's jealous because Minna wears my gift, not hers. But Minna can't wear a towel at her party.

A ribbon leads from each plate to a basket. The basket holds goodie bags — one for each of us. In every bag there are treats and a bracelet.

"They're friendship bracelets," Minna says. "I wish they were as beautiful as the one Lilly gave me."

Theresa scowls like a bulldog.

"This is awesome birthday cake," I say.

"Minna's grandma made the cake," her mom says. "And I decorated it."

Minna's dad grins. "And I made the icing," he says. "That was the toughest job. All those colours. Phew!"

Minna laughs. Her eyes shine. Piano lessons cost a lot of money and her parents have to work hard at their store. Usually they work on Saturdays, too, but not today. They wouldn't miss Minna's birthday.

5
It's the Thought
that Counts

Sara's mom comes to pick her up. Dana's parents come for her. The adults sit down for tea and cake.

"I think it's time I went home," I say to Minna. "Thank you for the party."

"Thank you for the bracelet," Minna says.

"You shouldn't wear that bracelet to school," Theresa says loudly. "You might lose it, and it cost a lot of money."

Theresa shouldn't talk about how

much the bracelet cost. It's none of her business.

Minna looks guilty. "I hope you didn't spend too much money on my present, Lilly." Minna knows we drive an old Chevy, too.

"Not all that much," I say. But fifteen dollars *is* a lot of money. I'd tell Minna how much it cost, but that would be tacky. It's the thought that counts. That's what the manager at the jewellery store said.

"It looks expensive," Minna says. "I don't want to lose it. I'm going to wear it at my next piano recital."

"I wouldn't if I were you," Theresa says.

"Why not?" Minna asks.

"I'll tell you later," Theresa says.

Theresa sure is jealous.

"I suppose it might fall down over my hand," Minna says. "But I can push it to the top of my arm. My new dress has cap sleeves. The bracelet will look great with it."

"That's why I bought it," I say. "To wear at concerts. The lights will shine on it and make it sparkle."

Minna smiles. I smile. Theresa does not smile.

6
The Gloomy Day

It's the day after Minna's party. The sky is low and grey. Rain, rain, rain all day. Boring! Pop and Macdonald are in the basement. They are making a birdhouse and a lot of noise. Actually, Pop is building the birdhouse. Macdonald mostly gets in the way. I go to help Mom bake cookies.

"Let's make gingerbread men," I say. "We can decorate them." I rattle through Mom's cookie cutters to find the one for gingerbread men.

"We're out of ginger," Mom says. "I used it up yesterday to make ginger-beef stir-fry."

I look through the kitchen window and see Minna and her grandma. I bet I know where they're headed — to the Garden Supermarket. If you walk, it isn't far through the walkway at the end of our street. If you drive, it's a long way around.

"There's Minna and her grandma, Mom. Can I go with them and buy ginger?" I ask.

"It's okay with me if it's okay with Minna's grandma," Mom says.

I run to the front door. "Grandma, Minna, please can I come with you? We need some ginger."

"Sure," Minna's grandma says. "We won't be long. I need onions. Wear your raincoat."

Minna looks grouchy. "You don't have to come," she says. "We'll bring the ginger for you." She doesn't look at me.

What's wrong with her? I thought she'd like me to go with them.

"Minna is in a bad mood," her grandma tells Mom. "Too much piano playing. Young bodies need exercise."

Mom gives me money for the ginger and we go. The rain has almost stopped. Minna trudges along behind her grandma and me. Her forehead is scrunched up into worry lines. I don't ask her what she's worried about. She won't tell me, not while she's in such a bad mood.

7
Friendship Bracelets

When we get to the supermarket, Minna says, "Go and buy your ginger, Lilly."

"Come with me," I say.

Minna shakes her head. "I'm going with Grandma." She follows her grandma to the veggie aisle.

I feel like crying. Why is Minna being so mean to me? I almost wish I hadn't given her that bracelet. If I hadn't, I'd still have five dollars in my piggy bank.

I find the ginger where Mom said it would be. I don't hurry back to Minna.

She won't be glad to see me.

On my way to the cashier I go through the section where they sell cards and candles. I like the way it smells. There, hung on a card, I see a bunch of friendship bracelets. The card is clipped to a shelf and I can't see the price. It must be behind the card. I know it isn't polite to look at how much they cost, but no one will see me. I look.

"Don't touch!" Minna's voice makes me jump. She sure sounds mad.

"I will if I want to." I'm mad now, too.

A clerk walks up the aisle.

"Can I help you?" she asks.

She doesn't sound as if she wants to help me. She sounds as if she thinks

I'm doing something wrong.

"Can you tell me how much these bracelets cost?" I ask.

"The price is up there." The clerk points to the shelf above the bracelets.

Now my cheeks feel hot because I didn't see it. The clerk goes on her way.

"She didn't have to be so grumpy about it," I say to Minna.

Minna frowns. "The store has to pay for the things people steal," she says. "Shoplifters steal from my mom and dad's store, too. It isn't fair. The clerk probably thought you were trying to steal a bracelet."

"Well, I wasn't," I say. "I don't want one of their crummy bracelets."

Then I remember that Minna gave

me a bracelet just like one of these. I wish I hadn't lost my temper. I don't really think the bracelet is crummy, but I can't say that. It will sound phony.

We walk home. Minna and I don't speak a word to one another.

8
Not Guilty

Today is Monday and we have to go to
school. Minna doesn't wait to walk
with me.

At recess I ask Theresa, "Why won't
Minna talk to me?"

"No one wants to talk to a
shoplifter." Theresa says. "Especially
the person who received the stolen
goods. People might think she stole
them, then she'd have to go to jail.
Maybe I shouldn't talk to you, either."

"What are you talking about?" I ask.
"What stolen goods?"

"What about the bracelet you gave

her?" Theresa asks.

"I didn't steal that!"

"Are you sure?" Theresa frowns at me.

"Of course I'm sure."

"My mom and I were in the mall last Saturday," Theresa says. "We passed the jewellery shop. I wanted to show the bracelet to my mom but it wasn't in the window. The manager saw us looking. He told my mom that someone stole it while his back was turned. He might have to pay for it out of his salary. That's not fair."

"Well, I didn't steal it," I say. "Did the manager say I did?"

"No," Theresa says. "But I saw you give it to Minna. And I know you couldn't afford to buy it."

"That wasn't the same bracelet," I say. "I bought mine at the Farmers' Market."

Davey comes to us. "Minna's crying," he says. "She's hiding under the slide, but I found her. I can't see, but I can hear better than most people. I think you are very mean to make Minna cry. I thought you were the coolest girl in the school, Lilly. So why do you steal things from the store? Cool girls don't steal."

9
Theresa's Fault

"But I don't steal things." I'm starting to get mad. "Does Minna think I stole her bracelet?"

"Yes," Davey says.

"It's your fault," I say to Theresa. "Why did you tell Minna that I stole her bracelet?"

"I had to," Theresa says. "What if Minna wears her bracelet when she plays the piano? The jewellery store manager might see her. He goes to music festivals, too, remember? He'll think Minna stole the bracelet and he'll tell the police. She'll go to jail."

"No, she won't," I say. "She'll tell the police I gave her the bracelet."

"I thought of that," Theresa says. "The police will know you can't afford that bracelet."

Davey nods. "And so you'll go to jail, too."

"I don't want you and Minna to go to jail," Theresa says. "My mom won't let me have jailbirds for friends."

"But I didn't steal the bracelet," I say. I'm getting really mad and a bit scared. Everyone seems to think I stole the bracelet. "I told you. I bought it at the Farmers' Market. I'm going to tell Minna."

Theresa and Davey follow me. Minna is still hiding under the slide. I wriggle in beside her. "Why did you

tell Davey I stole your bracelet?"

"I didn't," Minna says. "I wouldn't do that. He asked me why I was crying. I said someone I really like gave me an awesome bracelet, but she stole it, so now I can't wear it. I don't want her to get into trouble. And if I don't wear it, my friend will be hurt. We won't be friends anymore." She stops to sniff and wipe away her tears. "I didn't say the friend was you."

"I guessed," Davey says. He looks very pleased with himself. "I'm going to be a detective when I grow up."

"Minna," I say. "I didn't steal the bracelet. I bought it at the Farmers' Market."

"Prove it," Davey says.

10
It Really Is the Thought that Counts

After recess, instead of studying my spelling, I think about the bracelet. I decide to tell Minna how much I paid for it. So what if it isn't good manners to tell? Good manners aren't as important as your friend's happiness. After school, Theresa, Minna and I walk home together.

"My mom and I paid fifteen dollars for your bracelet, Minna," I say. "Mom paid ten dollars and I paid five. If you don't believe me, ask my mom."

"I believe you, Lilly," Minna says.

She gives me a big hug. "I should have known you wouldn't steal it."

Theresa stops walking. She gasps. "Fifteen dollars? I don't believe it. You can't buy gold and diamonds for fifteen dollars." She starts walking again, slowly. "D'you know what I think? I think it was the woman who sold you the bracelet. She stole it."

"She said she made it," I say.

"Maybe she wasn't telling the truth."

"There's only one thing to do," Minna says. "We'll take the bracelet to the manager of the jewellery store. He'll know if the bracelet is the one that was stolen. If it is, we'll give it back."

"But you won't have the bracelet

anymore," I point out.

Minna looks sad. "And you won't have your fifteen dollars anymore."

"I don't want to get the lady at the Farmers' Market in trouble," I say.

Theresa looks grim. "If she's innocent, she has nothing to fear."

We tell my mom what we want to do. She takes us to the jewellery store but she stays outside.

"Aren't you coming in with us?" I ask.

"I think you girls can handle this on your own," she says. "I'll be here if you need me."

My legs are shaking, even though I'm innocent. The manager takes the bracelet through a door at the back of the store. I can hardly breathe. He

comes back and lays the bracelet on the counter. My heart is going thump, thump. It's so loud I'm afraid he'll hear it.

"This is not the stolen bracelet. It's a copy. It isn't made of real gold, or real silver or real diamonds. These are clever imitations." He smiles at Minna. "But don't worry. When you wear it on stage no one will know the difference. Your bracelet will shine just like the real thing."

I sigh. "I should have known it wasn't real. It didn't cost enough."

"Price doesn't matter," Theresa says. "It's the thought that counts."

Minna smiles. "And every time I wear my bracelet, Lilly, I'll think of you."

Two more new novels in the *First Novels Series*!

Morgan Makes a Deal

Ted Staunton
Illustrated by Bill Slavin

A paper route is a lot more work than Morgan imagined, and when Aldeen tags along, there is double the work and triple the trouble. He comes up with a deal. If Aldeen and Charlie help deliver newspapers, he will give them the answers to their math homework. Morgan's helpers get top marks in math, he gets the cash for the route. It's a great plan … until Morgan's mother finds out. And since she has also been helping out, she wants to make sure that everyone gets a fair deal.

In this new story about Morgan and his friends, there is lots to learn about paper routes and friendships.

Robyn's Party in the Park

Hazel Hutchins
Illustrated by Yvonne Cathcart

When Robyn starts planning her birthday party, her mother makes just one rule: everyone in her class has to be invited. There are some kids she's not sure she wants to invite, including Jessica Johnston. In the end she takes Jessica's invitation to her at her home and Jessica breaks the news that she is having a party the same day, but *her* parents have ruled that she can only invite a few friends. Robyn isn't one of them.

In this story, Robyn takes the initiative to use this unexpected event to make new and better party plans.

Meet all the great kids in the *First Novels Series*!

Formac Publishing Company Limited
5502 Atlantic Street, Halifax, Nova Scotia B3H 1G4
Orders: 1-800-565-1975 Fax: 902-425-0166
www.formac.ca